To the wild adventurers of Studio Venture and Studio 78 Folies.
— R.B. & B.C.

I would like to thank Ramona Bădescu for working so closely with me, as well as MLGB and Max Hallinan for their wonderful insight into and suggestions on the translation. — CZB

www.enchantedlionbooks.com

First American edition published in 2014 by Enchanted Lion Books
351 Van Brunt Street, Brooklyn, NY 11231
Originally published in France by Albin Michel Jeunesse © 2012 as *Pomelo et la grande aventure*
Translated from the French by Claudia Bedrick
Translation copyright © 2014 Enchanted Lion Books
Copyright © 2014 by Enchanted Lion Books for the English-language edition
All rights reserved under International and Pan-American Copyright Conventions
A CIP record is on file with the Library of Congress
ISBN: 978-1-59270-158-2. Printed in December 2013 by Toppan Leefung

Pomelo's Big Adventure

Ramona Bădescu   Benjamin Chaud

ENCHANTED LION BOOKS

NEW YORK

Now that his dandelion is bare,
Pomelo has decided that it's time
to set out on his big adventure.

He begins by packing his knapsack.
He'll take his toothbrush, his knife-fork, his pillow,
an old photograph, some ribbon, pumpkin seeds,
a world map, a candle, matches, a pot, some shoes,
a head of garlic, a stone, crayons, a notebook, a good book,
his courage, and…Gigi the snail? No, not Gigi,
but some strawberries to quench his thirst
and some acorns for the road as well.

To give himself courage, Pomelo tells himself
that the most important thing is to have a good heart.
Then he leaves … is leaving … will leave …
But first he has to take a wee and a last look around.

He ties a ribbon to a stone and tosses it.
That's the direction in which he'll go.

He takes the route such as it is:
prickly, uphill, sticky, boring, surprising,
lively, and…lost in the distance.

Passing through mythic landscapes,
Pomelo is sure of one thing.

His paws are burning.

"Hey!" Suddenly someone gives an angry shout.
Someone who uses all kinds of words
Pomelo has never heard before and says things
like "my man," "cool," and "burn rubber."
Someone who talks and talks and talks…

By morning, Pomelo understands that going fast
means lightening his load. A lot.

VROOOOOOM! He's zooming through the big, wide world!

But wide-open spaces are much better with
a car that goes. How can this have happened?
Pomelo feels frustrated and upset.

Pomelo had thought that luck was smiling down on him,
but instead it's bad luck that's arrived. Only now does he realize
that the fast talker might have had something to do with it.

Pomelo feels like he wants to disappear.

He should never have decided to go on an adventure.

He wants to cry.

He wants a papa or a mama.

Or at least an umbrella.

Then he makes up his mind.
No! He's not going to cry.
Forward! March!
He stumbles. He picks himself up
and marches on.

We take many risks in life, of course,
but Pomelo seems to have plunged into
a world ruled by chance.

The next thing Pomelo knows, he's looking at
a big, gray shadow looming over a fire.
A shadow that welcomes him with, "Hello, my boy!"
and quickly puts a sausage on the grill for him.

Pomelo doesn't normally eat sausages but he eats this one.
It's good and warm.
The two sit together in silence looking up at the sky.

Then the big shadow says, "You see that bright star, my boy?
That star is watching over you, just like a Mamamelo."

He says nothing more and continues to eat his sausage.

When Pomelo opens his eyes, night has disappeared,
the fire has disappeared, and the stars have
disappeared. In the morning light, the big, gray shadow,
who has become Papamelo, is gathering wood nearby.

Pomelo learns to tie branches together, to chop,
to angle, to measure, and to sand. Then he transforms
all of that into a boat.

"It's time to leave," says Papamelo, and Pomelo thinks how that moment always seems to arrive. He also thinks he heard Papamelo say something else, like, "Go as far as you can," or "Go as fast as you can," but he's not sure. Already he's sailing away, and Papamelo is no more than a distant blur.

Suddenly the waves are getting bigger and bigger.
Pomelo feels like there's no longer anything to protect him.
His boat pitches and sways.

Inside Pomelo feels jiggly, like a heap of pudding on a plate.
He wants that feeling to go away.
What can he do to stop it?

Pomelo gazes up at the sky and at his star.
Now he knows that his star, his Mamamelo, is tenderly looking down on him.

Pomelo smiles. Although he's alone, he doesn't feel alone.
Now that he has his star, he'll never have to feel alone again.

Pomelo opens his eyes. At first, he can't see anything at all.
Slowly he realizes that it's no longer high tide
and that the waves are lapping joyfully against the sand.
The sky is blue through and through.
It also seems like he might have grown some hair.

Pomelo wonders if his adventure has changed him too much.
He also wonders who is looking back at him from the puddle.

For a moment, he thinks he's dreaming.

But Pomelo isn't dreaming!

Now he wonders what to call this odd creature that's a flower,
a mirror, and a ball of quills with saucer eyes all at the same time.
This creature that can remain as still as a stone for hours
but then runs off as fast as the wind.

What should he call a creature that can put
its head between its legs, stick out its tongue while
squinting, appear and disappear instantly,
and even get the better of a crab?

It's the first time that Pomelo has met someone so…so…
He doesn't know how to describe it but he wants to try.
To give himself courage, he looks out at the sea and
at the sky and toward the horizon.

"It…It looks like…" Again Pomelo looks into the sky.

"Like we're on a big adventure," concludes the Starfish,
whose eyes sparkle with the sunset and into
the twilight blue of the oncoming night.